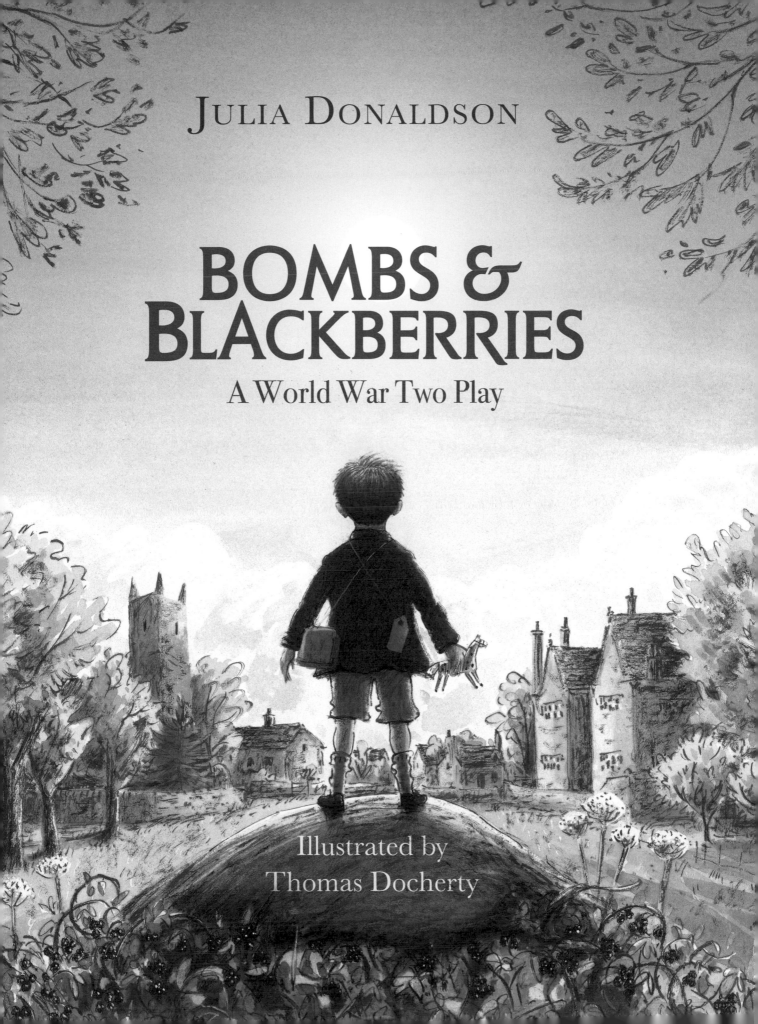

JULIA DONALDSON

BOMBS & BLACKBERRIES

A World War Two Play

Illustrated by
Thomas Docherty

First published in 2003 by Wayland
This edition published in 2018 by Hodder Children's Books

Text copyright © Julia Donaldson 2003
Illustrations copyright © Thomas Docherty 2018

Hodder Children's Books
An imprint of Hachette Children's Group
Part of Hodder & Stoughton
Carmelite House, 50 Victoria Embankment
London, EC4Y 0DZ

The right of Julia Donaldson to be identified as the author
and Thomas Docherty as the illustrator of this Work has been asserted by them
in accordance with the Copyright, Designs and Patents Act 1988.

A catalogue record of this book is available from the British Library.

ISBN: 978 1 444 93879 1

1 3 5 7 9 10 8 6 4 2

Printed in China

An Hachette UK Company
www.hachette.co.uk

FSC
www.fsc.org

MIX
Paper from
responsible sources
FSC® C104740

Hodder
Children's
Books

INTRODUCTION

It is September 1939. War has been declared, and a German invasion is feared. Millions of children from British towns are being herded to railway stations, to be taken to the greater safety of the countryside.

The play follows the fortunes of the Chivers family from Manchester during the first two years of the Second World War. Although the family and the other characters are fictional, the play is based on the facts of the Manchester evacuation and the Christmas Blitz of 1940.

The play can either be staged, or it can be read at home or in class. There are 29 speaking parts: 14 for girls, 14 for boys and one (the wireless voice) for either a girl or boy.

Additional children could appear in the railway carriage, street and playground scenes, joining in with the chants, games and songs.

The play can, however, be read in small groups, with some children taking more than one role.

Although the play has been divided into six scenes, the action moves from place to place within each scene. In total there are eleven locations: a railway carriage, the Chivers' home, a village hall, a playground, a casualty department, the garden of a stately home, a shop, a street, an air-raid shelter, a hospital ward and a field.

CAST

MANCHESTER PEOPLE

Name	Role
Mr Percy Chivers	Large
Mrs Hilda Chivers	Large
Stanley Chivers (aged 18)	Large
Doris Chivers, a nurse (aged 17)	Large
Elsie Chivers (aged 11)	Large
Jack Chivers (aged 9)	Large
Joey Chivers (aged 5)	Large

The Chivers Family

Name	Role
Mr Biggs	Medium
Brian Biggs (aged 10)	Large
Charlie Biggs (aged 8)	Medium
Mrs Dawson, a shopkeeper	Medium
Vera Dawson (aged 9)	Small
May Dawson (aged 8)	Small
Kenny Larkin (aged 10)	Small
Miss Oldham, a teacher	Medium

COUNTRY PEOPLE

Name	Role
Mrs Smiley, the parish clerk	Medium
Mrs Huggins	Medium
Sally Huggins (aged 11)	Medium
Farmer Gregg	Medium
Albert, the chauffeur at Kite Hall	Small
Miss Skelton, the housekeeper at Kite Hall	Medium
Eileen ⎫	Small
Norma ⎪ Children in the	Small
Harry ⎬ village school	Medium
George ⎭	Small

OTHER CHARACTERS

Name	Role
Luigi (aged 21), Italian prisoner of war	Medium
Paolo (aged 21), Italian prisoner of war	Medium
Nurse Christine, an army nurse	Medium
Wireless voice	Small

SCENE 1

FAREWELL, MANCHESTER, AUTUMN 1939

(Miss Oldham, Joey, Elsie, Jack, Doris, Mr Chivers, Mrs Chivers, Brian, Stanley; non-speaking parts: Charlie, Vera, May)

A RAILWAY CARRIAGE IN A MANCHESTER STATION

Seven Manchester children and their teacher, Miss Oldham, are squashed on to the seats. The children are Elsie, Jack and Joey Chivers; Brian and Charlie Biggs; Vera and May Dawson. They have labels on their coats, gas masks in boxes around their necks, and rucksacks in the luggage racks.

Miss Oldham: Ready, children? One, two, three, four!

Children: *(Singing)*

Fare-well, Man-ches-ter! No - ble town, fare - we-ell!

Here with loy - al - ty ev - 'ry breast can swell.

Where - so - e'er I roam, here, as in a home,

Ev - er, dear Lan-ca-shire, my heart shall dwell.

Joey: (*Standing up and looking out of window*)

    Our mum's crying! Elsie! Jack! Our mum's crying!

Elsie: Sit down, Joey.

Joey: Why is she crying? Doesn't she want us to have

    a holiday in the country?

Jack: Sit down!

Miss Oldham: Yes, sit down like everyone else, Joey. You've already said goodbye to

    your mum. (*Joey sits down. A whistle sounds.*)

Jack: We're off!

(*Joey jumps up again.*)

Joey: Bye-bye, Mum!

Miss Oldham: Sit down!

(*Joey takes no notice. The other children jump up and jostle each other at the window.*)

Children: Goodbye! Goodbye!

Miss Oldham: Sit down! *Sit down!*

(*The children sit down and "freeze".*)

THE CHIVERS' HOME

Mr Chivers enters, carrying a rusty helmet with a geranium growing in it.
He removes the geranium and starts to scrub the helmet. Enter Doris,
wearing a nurse's uniform.

Doris: (*Singing*) "Chew, chew, chew your bubblegum . . ."

    Oh, hello Dad. What are you doing?

Mr Chivers: What does it look like?

Doris: It looks like you're trying to kill that geranium.

    Put it back in the flowerpot, Dad.

Mr Chivers: That's no flowerpot. That's me helmet, that is.

Doris: Yes, I know, but it's been a flowerpot for years.

Mr Chivers: It did me for the last war, and it'll do me for this one.

Doris: Don't be daft, Dad! You're too old to fight.

Mr Chivers: That's as may be, but I don't want a lump of shrapnel in me skull
when I'm putting out fires, do I? Don't want a chimney pot braining me when
I'm digging folks out of the rubble.

Doris: What's that supposed to mean?

Mr Chivers: It means I'm joining the fire service.

(Enter Mrs Chivers.)

Doris: Hello, Mum. Are the kiddies away, then?

Mrs Chivers: Aye, they're away . . . and I nearly jumped on the train with them.
Our Joey's little face when they were singing that song! *(She sniffs and gets out her hanky.)*

Mr Chivers: They'll be all right, Hilda love.

Mrs Chivers: I just hope they'll stick together. I've told Elsie and Jack they must stick together and keep Joey with them.

Doris: Of course they'll stick together.

Mrs Chivers: It's so awful not knowing how long they'll be away. Suppose this war goes on as long as the last one?

Mr Chivers: It won't. We'll have Hitler licked in no time.

Mrs Chivers: What are you doing, Percy? Put that geranium back in the flowerpot.

Mr Chivers: It's not a flowerpot, it's a helmet. It did me for the last war and it'll do me for this one.

Mrs Chivers: Don't be stupid, Percy. They'll give you a new helmet. Honestly, you and your crackpot ideas!

Mr Chivers: Not crackpot, Hilda – crack*helmet!*

(Mr Chivers laughs at his own joke and exits. Mrs Chivers and Doris "freeze".)

THE RAILWAY CARRIAGE

Joey is holding a little wooden horse to the window and making clip-clop noises.

Joey: Look, Clopper, a station. What station was that, Elsie?

Elsie: I don't know. They've painted out all the names. It's to confuse the Germans.

Joey: I don't want the Germans to come.

Jack: It's all right, Joey. They won't get far. We'll set traps for them.

Brian: Don't talk so loud, Jack Chivers. Some of them are here already. They're all disguised as nuns and monks.

Jack: Don't be daft, Brian Biggs. Can you see any nuns and monks on this train? It's full of schoolkids.

Brian: What about the guard? He could be a spy. He's got yellow hair.

Jack: So what?

Brian: So, the Germans have all got yellow hair. Don't you know anything, Jack Chivers?

Jack: Yes, I know that you're a daftie.

Miss Oldham: Pipe down, you two. And pull your socks up, Jack.

    We're nearly there. The tidier you look, the sooner you'll get chosen.

Joey: *(Still holding his horse to the window)* Horses! Look, Clopper, horses!

    They're going to fight in the war, like you!

Brian: No, they're not! You don't get horses in the war.

Joey: Yes, you do. Our dad said so. He was in the war.

Brian: That was a different war.

Joey: Well, Clopper's going to be in this war. Clopper's a war horse.

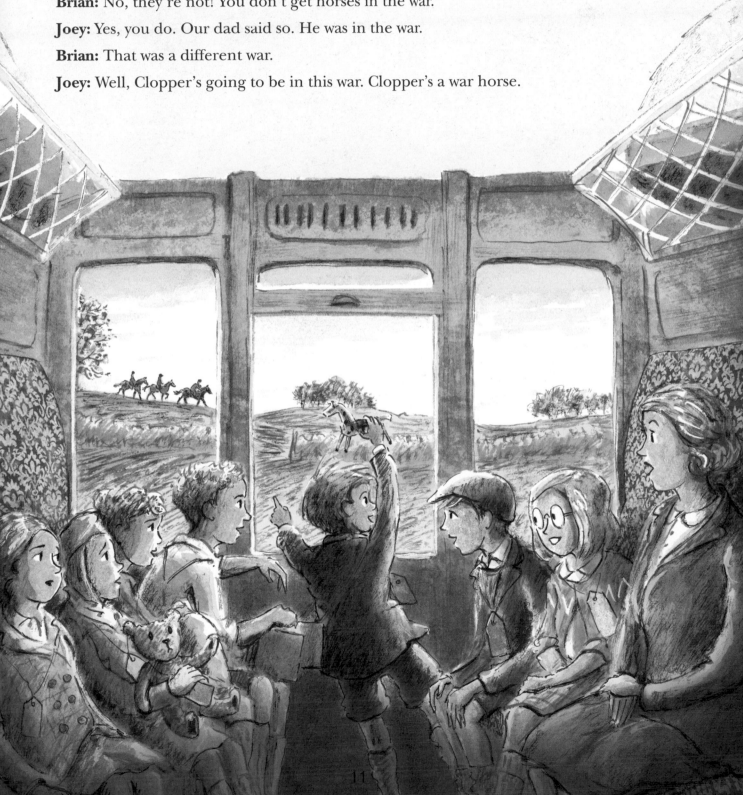

Brian: *(To Jack)* Your little brother's as daft as you.

Miss Oldham: Don't start that again, you two. How about another song, everyone?

How about "Run, rabbit, run?"

Children: *(Singing)*

Run, rab-bit, run, rab-bit, run, run, run.

Don't give the far-mer his fun, fun, fun.

He'll get by with-out his rab-bit pie. So

run, rab-bit, run, rab-bit, run, run, run.

(The children "freeze".)

THE CHIVERS' HOME

Mrs Chivers: It feels so quiet without them.

Doris: Come on, Mum, you were always on at them to keep the noise down.

Mrs Chivers: I know – and now I miss it.

(Enter Stanley Chivers, singing.)

Stanley: "There's something about a soldier, there's something about . . ."

Oh, hello, Mum.

Mrs Chivers: Why aren't you at work, Stan?

Stanley: I didn't go in to Metrovick. I've been down to the recruiting office.

Mrs Chivers: What? You've never joined up! *(Sitting down)* Oh, Stan, what a moment to pick!

Doris: Did you pass the medical, Stan?

Stanley: Aye, I'm fighting fit! I'm off tomorrow!

Doris: Tomorrow! What, off to France?

Stanley: No, not to France. I've got to go to a training centre first.

Mrs Chivers: Oh, Stan, why wouldn't you wait to be called up? After all, you'd be helping just as much by staying on in your job. We all know Metrovick is making weapons and suchlike.

Stanley: Look, Mum, I've had an idea. You could get a job with Metrovick yourself! They're opening that new machine shop next month. They'll be looking for tons of workers.

Doris: What are they going to be making, Stan?

Stanley: It's hush-hush.

Mrs Chivers: I might just do that. It'll get me away from this hush-hush house.

SCENE 2

THE "VACKIES", AUTUMN 1939

(Farmer Gregg, Mrs Smiley, Joey, Jack, Sally, Elsie, Mrs Huggins, Miss Oldham, Vera, May, Albert, Eileen, George, Norma, Harry, Charlie, Brian)

THE VILLAGE HALL

Miss Oldham, Elsie, Jack, Joey, Brian, Charlie, Vera and May are sitting around looking tired. Mrs Smiley, the parish clerk, is bustling about. Enter Farmer Gregg.

Farmer Gregg: Have you got three strong, sturdy lads?

Mrs Smiley: This isn't a cattle market, Mr Gregg.

Farmer Gregg: I know it's not – I've got plenty of cows. It's cow*boys* I'm short of!
    (He points at Brian and Charlie.) These two will do. *(Pointing at Jack)* And maybe this one
    with the tumbledown socks. I bet you lads don't even know where milk comes from.

Joey: I do! It comes from a jug.

Farmer Gregg: See what I mean? Right, you three, you come along with me.

Jack: Excuse me, mister . . . I can't. I promised our mum we'd stay together.

Farmer Gregg: I'll just take the two, then.

Mrs Smiley: Very well. I'm sure you'll be happy on the farm, boys. The fresh air
    will do you good.

(Brian and Charlie exit with Farmer Gregg. Sally Huggins enters, out of breath, with a bag of apples.)

Sally: Hello, Mrs Smiley. I've brought some apples for the vackies.

Mrs Smiley: You shouldn't call them that, Sally – but I'm sure they'll like the apples.

(Sally hands out the apples.)

Sally: *(To Elsie)* What's your name?

Elsie: Elsie.

Sally: Here's an apple, Elsie. It's from our garden.

Elsie: Thank you. Do you want a currant bun? *(She gets one out of her bag.)* Sorry it's a bit squashed.

Sally: Mmm, it's scrummy.

(Enter Mrs Huggins.)

Mrs Smiley: Hello, Mrs Huggins. It's a couple of girls for you, isn't it?

Mrs Huggins: Yes, please.

Sally: Can we have Elsie, Mum?

Mrs Huggins: Would you like to come with us, Elsie?

Elsie: I can't. I promised I'd stick with my brothers.

Miss Oldham: How about these two sisters, Vera and May Dawson? Nobody's chosen them yet because May's got asthma.

Mrs Huggins: Poor little soul. Would you like to come and share with Sally, girls?

Vera and May: Yes please!

Sally: But they're too little, Mum. I want Elsie!

Mrs Huggins: You'll see Elsie at school, Sally. Ready, you two? Don't forget your gas masks.

Miss Oldham: See you in school, girls!

(Vera and May exit with Sally and Mrs Huggins.)

Mrs Smiley: The fresh air will do them good.

Joey: What about us?

Mrs Smiley: Don't worry. I'm sure we'll find someone.

(Enter Albert.)

Mrs Smiley: Ah, good afternoon, Albert. Did Lady Ingleby send you?

Albert: Yes. She said she'd take any that were left over.

Mrs Smiley: You lucky children! You're going to be staying in Kite Hall. It's a very grand house. There's even a billiard room, isn't there, Albert?

Albert: That's where they're going to be sleeping.

Miss Oldham: Well I never! You'll be such toffs you won't want to know your old teacher! Pull your socks up, Jack! Goodbye, and be good.

Children: Goodbye. *(The children follow Albert out.)*

Mrs Smiley: The fresh air will do them good.

THE PLAYGROUND OF THE VILLAGE SCHOOL

Harry, Eileen, George, Norma and Sally run on. Harry stands apart from the others.

Eileen, George and Norma: Farmer, farmer, may I cross your field?

Harry: Yes, if you're wearing red.

(George takes a step forwards.)

Eileen, George and Norma: Farmer, farmer, may I cross your field?

Harry: Yes, if you're wearing black.

(Eileen takes a step forwards.)

Harry: You're not wearing black, Eileen Miller.

Eileen: What colour do you think my gas mask box is, then? It's made of blackout material.

(Enter Elsie, Vera, May, Charlie and Joey. Joey sits sadly down with his horse. The rest approach the country children.)

Vera: Can we play?

Harry: No, you can't. No vackies allowed.

Charlie: Why not?

Eileen: Because you're from Manchester.

George: You're dirty.

Norma: You've all got head lice.

May: No, we have not!

Harry: Well, you can't play anyway.

Charlie: I'm going to get my big brother on to you. Brian! Brian!

(Enter Brian and Jack.)

Charlie: That boy says we can't play. He says we're all dirty.

Harry: No, I never. It was George who said that.

George: No, I never. It was Eileen.

Brian: Their game looks stupid, anyway. Me and Jack are playing spies. You can
play with us, Charlie.

(Exit Brian, Jack and Charlie.)

Sally: I vote the Manchester girls can play with us.

Elsie: I'm only playing if my little brother can play with us.

Joey: I don't want to.

Norma: Let's get a move on – playtime's nearly over.

Children: Farmer, farmer, may I cross your field?

Harry: Yes, if you've got head lice!

(No one steps forward. The bell goes. The children run off, some of them laughing. Elsie leads Joey off, with her arm round him.)

SCENE 3

THE BLACKOUT, AUTUMN – WINTER 1939

(Mrs Chivers, Mr Chivers, Doris, Mr Biggs)

THE CHIVERS' HOME.

Enter Mrs Chivers, with a letter, and Mr Chivers.

Mrs Chivers: There's another letter from our Elsie.

Mr Chivers: Let's have a read. *(Mr Chivers takes the letter and reads aloud.)*

Dear Mum and Dad,

I am having a nice time in the country. I have
only seen Lady Ingleby twice. Mostly we just see the housekeeper,
Miss Skelton. Yesterday, me and Sally picked lots of field mushrooms
and her mother cooked them.

Mrs Chivers: Oh, no! What if they were them poisonous ones?

Mr Chivers: Of course they weren't. Be quiet and listen:

> . . . Jack got in a fruit fight with some boys from the village. Miss Skelton was cross with him. Joey is still a bit sad. I think he is homesick.
>
> With love from Elsie.

Mrs Chivers: Poor Joey. I've a good mind to have them back.

Mr Chivers: No, Hilda, it's too dangerous.

Mrs Chivers: Dangerous? Come off it, Percy. How many German planes have you seen? How many fires have you put out?

Mr Chivers: If we go through all that again we'll both be late for work.

> *(Picking up his helmet)* Come on.

Mrs Chivers: If you ask me, the real danger isn't Hitler – it's the blackout.

(Exit Mr and Mrs Chivers.)

THE CASUALTY DEPARTMENT OF A MANCHESTER HOSPITAL

Enter Doris, in her nurse's uniform, and Mr Biggs.

Doris: Hello, Mr Biggs. The doctor says you've broken your collarbone.

Mr Biggs: Aye. Blinking blackout!

Doris: I'll put a sling on it for you. *(Doris bandages Mr Biggs while they talk.)*
You're Brian and Charlie's dad, aren't you? How are they doing on
the farm?

Mr Biggs: They're getting on fine. But you'll never guess what the farmer's been getting
our Brian to do.

Doris: Milk the cows?

Mr Biggs: No – paint white stripes on them! It's because a cow got knocked down by a car the other week. They have the blinking blackout in the country, too. Pointless, if you ask me.

Doris: So, what happened to you?

Mr Biggs: Well, I were down the Shambles. Do you know the Shambles?

Doris: Yes, it's that old area, isn't it?

Mr Biggs: Aye, all steps and twisty alleyways. I went down the Shambles for a couple of pints.

Doris: Just a couple?

Mr Biggs: Well, maybe three or four. Anyway, when I comes out, it's pitch black. No moon at all. And I'd forgotten me torch. Can't get into the habit of using the things. So there I am, hurrying to catch me tram, and I slips up. I reckon I chose the wrong pub.

Doris: Why?

Mr Biggs: It were called The Slip Inn!

SCENE 4

TRICKLING HOME, SPRING – SUMMER 1940

(Elsie, Jack, Joey, Miss Skelton, Mrs Dawson, Mrs Chivers, Brian, Kenny, Stanley)

The garden at Kite Hall

A sheet is pegged out on a washing line.

Elsie: *(Offstage)* Seven, eight, nine, ten. I'm coming!
(Jack hides behind the sheet. Joey follows him, holding Clopper.)
Jack: You can't hide here. This is my place.
Joey: Oh, go on, Jack! Elsie's coming.
Jack: All right, then.

(There are footsteps. Miss Skelton, the housekeeper, removes the sheet and stands holding it.)

Joey: It's not Elsie – it's Miss Skelton.

Jack: Good afternoon, Miss Skelton.

Miss Skelton: It may be a good afternoon, but it wasn't a very good night, was it?

Jack: What do you mean?

Miss Skelton: I think your little brother knows what I mean. It was another *wet* night, wasn't it, Joey?

Joey: Yes, Miss. I'm sorry, Miss.

Miss Skelton: Do you think I like washing your wet sheets every day while you run about playing hide-and-seek?

Joey: It's not hide-and-seek, it's prisoners and guards. Me and Jack are escaped prisoners.

Miss Skelton: You've got every convenience at Kite Hall. An indoor flush toilet, running hot water . . . you don't have those at home, do you?

Joey: No, Miss Skelton.

Miss Skelton: So why don't you make use of them? Are you just too lazy to get out of bed?

Jack: It's not Joey's fault, Miss Skelton. He doesn't want to wet the bed. He's just homesick.

Miss Skelton: Well, there's a cure for every sickness, and I think I've worked out a cure for this one. Show me that little horse of yours, Joey. *(Joey holds the horse out and Miss Skelton takes it.)* You're fond of it, aren't you?

Joey: Yes, Miss Skelton. Can I have Clopper back, please?

Miss Skelton: You can have Clopper back in the morning – as long as your bed's dry.

(Miss Skelton exits with the sheet and the horse. Elsie runs on.)

Elsie: Found you! Your turn to be the guard, Jack. Come on, Joey!

Joey: I'm not playing any more.

(Joey walks away sadly, and Jack and Elsie follow him.)

A GROCERY SHOP IN MANCHESTER

Mrs Dawson is behind the counter. Enter Mrs Chivers.

Mrs Dawson: Hello, Mrs Chivers. What can I do for you?

Mrs Chivers: Just the usual. Here's our ration books. *(Handing them to Mrs Dawson)*
Give us a tin of Spam, too – it'll jazz up the vegetable pie.

Mrs Dawson: *(Starting to weigh out sugar, butter and bacon)* How about the vegetables?
Have you got them?

Mrs Chivers: Yes – Percy's been growing them on top of the shelter. Digging for victory,
like it says in the posters.

Mrs Dawson: *(Handing the packages to Mrs Chivers)* Here you are, then – sugar, butter, bacon.
And here's your dried egg.

Mrs Chivers: How I hate the stuff!

Mrs Dawson: Me, too. The funny thing is, Vera and May like it. They've been
having fresh farm eggs all these months but now they prefer the powdered kind.

Mrs Chivers: Are they back home, then?

Mrs Dawson: Aye, we fetched them back at the weekend. I don't reckon Hitler's going to bother with little old Britain after all. I'm surprised you let your kiddies stay at Kite Hall. Vera's been telling us about Joey.

Mrs Chivers: What about him?

Mrs Dawson: Well . . . I mean, our May wet the bed for a couple of weeks, too, but Sally's mother was very understanding. That Miss Skelton sounds a right so-and-so. Fancy taking away his little horse every time he does it!

Mrs Chivers: I didn't know anything about all this. Elsie and Jack never said anything in their letters.

Mrs Dawson: No, well, maybe they're not free to. That Skelton woman probably reads every word they write.

Mrs Chivers: That does it – they're coming home!

(Mrs Chivers takes her shopping and exits. Mrs Dawson follows.)

A MANCHESTER STREET

Enter Jack and Joey, Brian and Charlie, and Kenny.

Brian: Let's play convoys.

Kenny: How do you play that?

Brian: You all have to line up. Littlest one at the front – that's you, Joey. Now you all squat down. You're a line of tanks. You've got to move forward slowly, and I'm going to bomb you. I'll wrap some sand in my hanky for the bomb.

(Jack, Joey, Charlie and Kenny move forward. Stanley Chivers enters, in uniform, looking very tired. No one notices him. Brian throws the "bomb". It lands near Kenny.)

Brian: You've been bombed, Kenny. You're out.

Kenny: That's not fair. It didn't hit me.

Brian: No, but it landed near you. It could have exploded and killed you.

Kenny: No, it couldn't.

Stanley: I'm afraid it could. I've seen that happen.

Jack: Stan! *(He turns to the others)* That's my big brother!

Joey: Stan! Stan! Why are you back? Have we won the war?

(Joey and Jack run up to Stanley. Brian, Charlie and Kenny cluster round.)

Stanley: No, Joey, we haven't. Not yet.

Kenny: Where have you been?

Stanley: Dunkirk. That's in France.

Joey: Did you come back in a big battleship?

Stanley: No – in a little French fishing boat. Is Mum home?

Joey: No, she's out at Metrovick.

Jack: She works there now, like you used to. She says she doesn't know
what they're making, but I reckon it's a new bomber.

Brian: Shut up, Jack! I keep telling you, walls have ears.

Joey: Do you want to play convoys, Stan?

Stanley: No, I've had enough war for a while. I just want my bed.

*(The game breaks up, with Stanley, Jack and Joey going one way, and Brian,
Charlie and Kenny going the other.)*

SCENE 5

THE CHRISTMAS BLITZ, WINTER 1940–1941

(Mr Chivers, Joey, Elsie, Mrs Chivers, Jack, the wireless voice, Doris, Mr Biggs, Brian, Charlie, Nurse Christine, Stanley)

THE CHIVERS' HOME

It is 22 December 1940. Enter Mrs Chivers with a tray of mince pies, and Mr Chivers with his helmet. Elsie and Jack carry in a Christmas tree, followed by Joey. Jack starts to wrap presents in brown paper, and Elsie starts to decorate the Christmas tree.

Mr Chivers: That Christmas tree looks grand, Elsie.

Joey: Let's hang Clopper up! He can be Father Christmas's reindeer.

Elsie: All right, then. Pass us the string, Jack.

(Elsie ties some string round Clopper and hangs him on the tree.)

Mrs Chivers: *(Putting the mince pies in the oven)* I'm warning you all – there won't be a cake this year. I've used up the last of the sugar in the mince pies.

Mr Chivers: Never mind, love. Christmas will still be Christmas, cake or no cake.

Mrs Chivers: It's not really the cake I'm going to miss. It's our Stanley.

Jack: At least we saw him in the summer, Mum.

Mrs Chivers: Aye, but then he was off again to Egypt as quick as you can say Jack Robinson.

Mr Chivers: Don't worry about Stan. I bet he's sitting on top of a pyramid, toasting us all.

Cheerio, everyone – see you all in the morning!

(Mr Chivers puts his helmet on and exits.)

Mrs Chivers: Let's put the wireless on – maybe there'll be some nice carols.

(She switches it on.)

The wireless voice: A town in the north-west of England was heavily bombed last night.

Mrs Chivers: Oh, no! That's really cheered me up! *(She switches the wireless off.)*

Jack: Which town was it, Mum?

Mrs Chivers: Liverpool. The fires were so bad that half the Manchester brigade had to go and help out. They're still there. That's why your dad's got to do this extra duty tonight.

(Enter Doris, looking glamorous.)

Elsie: You look nice, Doris.

Doris: What do you think of my lipstick?

Elsie: It looks good – but I thought you said you'd no lipstick left?

Doris: I haven't – this is beetroot juice!

Jack: Where are you off to, Doris?

Doris: I'm going to a party at the Eccles first aid post.

(The air-raid siren sounds.)

Doris: Oh, no! An air raid – that's just what I need.

Mrs Chivers: I doubt it'll last long. They're just passing over on their way to Liverpool. Right, come on, kiddies. Doris, turn off the oven, will you? Elsie, fetch us down a couple of extra blankets – it's going to be a cold night.

(There is a knock on the door. Doris opens it. Mr Biggs, Brian and Charlie are standing there.)

Doris: Hello, Mr Biggs.

Mr Biggs: We were just wondering, like – do you have any room in your shelter? Ours is flooded.

Mrs Chivers: Is it just the three of you?

Mr Biggs: Aye, my Betty's on duty at the rest centre.

Mrs Chivers: I daresay we can squeeze you in. Ready, everyone? *(They all exit.)*

THE AIR-RAID SHELTER IN THE CHIVERS' GARDEN

Mrs Chivers, Doris, Elsie, Jack, Joey, Mr Biggs, Brian and Charlie are inside it. Several hours have passed. There are sounds of aircraft and gunfire. A plane passes directly overhead.

Jack: That was a Stuka.

Brian: No, it wasn't – it was a Heinkel.

(There is the sound of a bomb exploding.)

Doris: That was close!

Mr Biggs: Come on, let's have another song.

(Mr Biggs starts to sing and the others join in.)

Joey: Where's Clopper?

Elsie: He's on the Christmas tree – don't you remember?

Joey: *(Going towards the door)* I'm going to get him.

Jack: Don't be daft, Joey.

Doris: Pass us your book, Joey – I'll read you another story.

Joey: I don't want a story. I want Clopper.

Charlie: Can we have a peep outside, Dad?

Mr Biggs: *(To Mrs Chivers)* What do you think? Shall we let them?

Mrs Chivers: All right, then, but put out the torches, everyone.

(Mr Biggs opens the door and they peer out.)

Charlie: The sky's all red.

Elsie: What's that on the roof?

Mr Biggs: By gum! It's a parachute! Keep back, everyone.

(Exit Mr Biggs.)

Joey: Where's he going?

Brian: There's a German landed on the roof. Dad's going to catch him.

Charlie: I can't see anyone on the roof.

Elsie: What's that box thing that's dangling down?

Joey: Is it the German's suitcase?

Jack: What? Where? *(He jostles to the front.)* There isn't a parachutist –
    that's a parachute bomb!

Brian: Dad! Stop! Stop!

Mrs Chivers: Mr Biggs!

Doris: Come back!

Charlie: It's a bomb!

(Mr Biggs comes back into view. As he approaches the shelter, there is a deafening explosion.)

AN ARMY HOSPITAL IN EGYPT

It is January 1941. Stanley Chivers, who has been wounded, is in bed. Nurse Christine, an army nurse, enters.

Nurse Christine: You're a lucky chappie, Gunner Chivers. You've got two letters. They've been forwarded from HQ. Shall I sit you up?

Stanley: Just call me Stan. *(He takes the letters.)* Ta. This one's from my mum. *(He starts to read.)*

Dear Stan,

I hope you are keeping safe in Egypt . . .

Oh, no!

Nurse Christine: What's the matter?

Stanley: They've been bombed out. They're in a rest home. All except my sister Elsie. She's gone to stay with her friend Sally in the country. It sounds terrible – listen to this. *(He reads)*

There were Christmas cards scattered all over the garden. Joey was upset about the tree and the presents getting burned – and that little horse you made for him.

Nurse Christine: Poor little thing. Did the fire brigade get there all right?

Stanley: I think so. Yes. Here's what she says: *(He reads)*

> Your dad's lot came, though not as quick as they might – there were that many fires all over the city. Doris's hospital was bombed. One bomb fell down a chimney into a ward full of patients but Doris's friend put it out by covering it with sand.

Nurse Christine: Good for her! Was Doris on duty, too?

Stanley: No, she was supposed to be going to a party. By golly, listen to this: *(He reads)*

> Thank goodness she didn't make it, because there was a bomb and twelve people were killed. Our Doris is a bit down in the dumps, but I daresay she'll snap out of it. Hoping for good news of you soon.
>
> Your loving Mother

Oh, no. *(He lies back in bed.)*

Nurse Christine: At least they're all alive, Stan.

Stanley: I know – but now they'll have got the telegram about my leg.

How are they going to feel about that?

Nurse Christine: Shall I read you your other letter?

Stanley: Yes, please. I think it's from Jack.

Nurse Christine: Here we go, then. *(She reads)*

Dear Stan,

I hope you are still beating the Italians in Egypt. We have had an exciting time. Our house got bombed, and so did loads of others. Me and Brian Biggs have collected tons of shrapnel. Mr Biggs got a bit burned by a parachute bomb, but he is more fed up about The Slip Inn getting destroyed. Metrovick got bombed, too, so we could all see what they were making. It was a new bomber, just like I said – a bomber called the 'Manchester'!

With love from Jack

That was a bit jollier.

Stanley: That's kids for you – the war's a big adventure to them.

Nurse Christine: You're not much more than a kid yourself, Stan.

Stanley: Well, I don't feel like one any more.

SCENE 6

PRISONERS OF WAR, AUTUMN 1941

(Elsie, Sally, Luigi, Paolo, Farmer Gregg, Kenny, Joey, Charlie, Brian, Jack, Doris, Mrs Smiley, Mrs Huggins)

A COUNTRY FIELD

Elsie and Sally are collecting rosehips.

Elsie: I've never tasted rosehip syrup. We never had it when we were little.

Sally: I don't like it much. But it's good for babies.

Elsie: I reckon we've picked enough for an army of babies.

Sally: We'll be getting medals from Mr Churchill.

Luigi and Paolo: *(Offstage, singing)*

"Una rosa da Vienna, Una piccola rosa . . ."

Elsie: Who's that singing?

Sally: I don't know. It sounds foreign. *(They peep offstage.)*

Elsie: Look! It's two men. They're picking Farmer Gregg's apples.

Sally: Do you think they're German invaders?

Elsie: I don't know . . . I thought Hitler had given up on that idea.

Sally: They've seen us! Shall we run?

Elsie: No – they look quite friendly.

(Enter Luigi and Paolo with baskets of apples.)

Luigi: Buongiorno!

Sally: I think they *are* German.

Paolo: No. No German. Italiano.

Elsie: They're Italian. They've not got any guns.

Paolo: No guns. Prisoners.

Luigi: Very nice prison. Sun, trees. No walls.

Paolo: You want apple?

Sally: No, thank you.

Luigi: Me – Luigi. My friend – Paolo.

Elsie: I'm Elsie. This is my friend Sally.

Luigi: Elsie. Sally. Very nice names. Very nice girls.

Paolo: You like pupina?

Sally: Pupina – what's that? *(Paolo produces a wooden doll.)* Oh, it's a doll. That's nice.

Paolo: I make it. Wood, knife.

Elsie: That's really clever.

Paolo: I make for my sister. But you can have.

Elsie: It's all right, Paolo. Me and Sally are too old for dolls. Keep it for your little sister.

Luigi: You have sister also?

Elsie: Not a little one – a big one. But she's in Manchester. Big town.

Luigi: Your big sister pretty like you?

Elsie: She's prettier than me! *(She laughs.)*

Luigi: Happy like you?

Elsie: I don't know. She always used to be happy. But then some of her friends got killed in the war. I think she's still sad about that.

Paolo: She come here. Sky, trees. Very nice. She happy again.

Sally: That's a good idea, Elsie. Why don't I ask Mum if Doris can come for a holiday? Maybe Joey could come, too. You and me could camp in the garden.

(Enter Farmer Gregg.)

Farmer Gregg: What's all this, then? You two are supposed to be picking apples, not chatting up the girls.

41

Sally: Don't be cross with them, Mr Gregg. Me and Elsie have got to go now. Goodbye, Luigi! Goodbye, Paolo!

Luigi: Arrivederci!

(They all exit.)

A MANCHESTER STREET

Enter Jack, Brian, Charlie, Joey and Kenny.

Kenny: "Eeny, meeny, Mussolini, Eeny, meeny, out!" You're an Italian, Joey.

Joey: I don't want to be.

Kenny: You've got to be. It's desert sands. You can't play desert sands without any Italians.

Charlie: I'm being Mussolini. Don't you want to be in my army, Joey?

Joey: No! I'm not being Italian! I hate Italians! *(He runs off.)*

Brian: Your brother's such a baby, Jack. You'd never think he was seven.

Jack: I know. But it's because of our big brother. It was the Italians who gave Stan his wooden leg.

Kenny: My uncle's got two wooden legs.

Brian: No, he has not, Kenny Larkin.

Charlie: Anyway, are we still playing desert sands?

Jack: Let's play it on the bombsite.

(They all run off.)

SCENE VI

THE COUNTRY FIELD

Enter Doris, Joey, Elsie, Sally, Mrs Huggins and Mrs Smiley with a picnic basket. They spread out a rug and sit down.

Doris: This blackberry jam is lovely. I do like a picnic!

Mrs Smiley: I can't get over how Joey's grown. Well, Joey, is it nice being back in the country?

Joey: Yes, Mrs Smiley.

Mrs Smiley: How about staying on? I'm sure Farmer Gregg would take you in. The fresh air would do you good.

Joey: No, thank you.

Mrs Huggins: I think he's scared of bumping into that Miss Skelton.

Doris: So, Elsie, what about this surprise you were on about?

Elsie: It's coming soon.

Sally: Here it comes!

(Sally points at Luigi and Paolo who enter with a basket.)

Luigi: Good afternoon.

Elsie: *(Proudly)* Buongiorno! That's "good day" in Italian. This is Luigi and this is Paolo. They're Italian prisoners. This is my little brother Joey, and this is my big sister Doris.

Doris: Hello, there!

Elsie: Say hello, Joey.

(Joey pretends not to hear.)

Mrs Huggins: Maybe he's shy.

Paolo: We bring plums. Many plums.

Luigi: And flowers. *(Luigi gives a bunch of wild flowers to Doris.)*

Doris: Thank you. They're beautiful.

Paolo: Your sister tell me you nurse. Now I want to be ill. I go to your hospital.

Joey: You can't. They don't let Italians in.

Doris: Don't be silly, Joey.

Sally: Doris's hospital got bombed, didn't it, Doris?

Doris: Yes, but it's been repaired now.

Luigi: War is sad. Many bombs. Many people kill. Me – two brothers die.

Mrs Huggins: I am sorry, Luigi.

Paolo: We no want to fight. Our leader, he want. We no want.

Mrs Smiley: It's a sorry business. Here, have a jam sandwich.

Luigi: Thank you. Very good bread. Good, like Italian bread.

Paolo: I have a present for you, Joey. *(He brings a jointed horse out of the basket of plums)*
Your sister tell me you like horses. I make for you. *(Paolo holds the horse out to Joey, who doesn't take it.)*

Doris: It's lovely! You are clever, Paolo.

(Paolo beams.)

Paolo: Is a dancing horse. I pull string, he dance.
(Paolo demonstrates. The others laugh.)

Doris: Say thank you, Joey.

Joey: *(Taking the horse)* Thank you.

Paolo: My town – Siena. Many horses – how you say, running quick, quick, quick?

Elsie: Racing? Horse racing?

Paolo: Yes. Horse racing. War finish, you come to Siena, Joey. Bring sisters.

Doris: I sometimes wonder if it will ever finish.

Luigi: Yes, yes. It finish.

Sally: When it does, I know what I want – a pound of flying saucers.

Elsie: *(Explaining to Paolo and Luigi)* They're a kind of sweet. I want a pound of pear drops.

Joey: I want a pound of liquorice bootlaces.

Doris: A drawer full of stockings will do me. How about you, Paolo?

Paolo: Pasta! Big, big – a mountain!

Luigi: For me, pizza – big, like horse-race place!

Mrs Smiley: A nice pleated skirt for me.

Mrs Huggins: And I'll have a crate of bananas!

Everyone: Mmmmmm!

Doris: There's a song about that.

(Doris starts to sing and the English people join in. The Italians begin to catch on, and by the end of the song Joey is dancing the horse about.)

Everyone: *(They sing the song twice)*

YES! We have no ba - na - nas —————— We have no ba -

na - nas to - day —————— We've string beans and HON-ions, cab-

BAH-ges and scal-lions And all kinds of fruit and say —————

—— We have an old fash-ioned to - MAH-to ——————

Long Is - land po - TAH - to —————— But YES! we

have no ba - na - nas —————— We have no ba - nas to-

day.

THE END

ABOUT THE PLAY

STAGING

There is no need for an elaborate production; it is probably more effective to keep props and scenery to a minimum.

The washing line in Scene 4 could be used at other points in the play to peg backcloths or props. The Christmas tree in Scene 5 could be made of paper or fabric and pegged on the line.

The children who are acting could also be scene shifters. For instance, the railway carriage in Scene 1 could be created by eight chairs which the actors later lift and scatter around to create the village hall at the beginning of Scene 2.

There are several sound effects in the play: the noises made by trains, planes and bombs, and the twittering of birds in the countryside. Children could either compile a soundtrack or make the noises with instruments or voices.

Scene changes could be indicated by sounds or music. For instance, at the beginning of the scene around the Christmas tree, the characters could enter humming a carol. Alternatively, a child could beat a gong or drum to indicate a scene change.

If lighting is to be used, a blackout at the "cliffhanger" ending of the air-raid scene would be effective.

COSTUME

Costumes can be kept simple, too. Most of the characters are quite poor, so some of the clothes could be patched.

Everyone was required to carry a gas mask during the war, so both town and country people should have boxes or bags on strings round their necks.

The schoolboys should wear shorts, not long trousers, and girls' and women's skirts should be knee-length.
Mr Chivers' helmet could be made of papier mâché.

The two nurses, Albert the chauffeur and soldier Stan do not have to be in full uniform; indications such as appropriate headgear will be enough. Stan could wear pyjamas in Scene 5.

The two Italian prisoners of war could wear boiler suits, and the housekeeper, Miss Skelton, could be dressed in an overall.

Enjoy yourselves!